RECKONING WITH THE Vector Axe

SHRIKANTA jilla

———— ★·☆·★ ————
Dedicated to amma and pappa.
———— ★·☆·★ ————

CONTents

Author's Note	(i)
Acknowledgments	(iii)
Character's List	(v)
Preface	(ix)

I-The Boy's Past	1
II-Andrew is Attacked	6
III-Devotes Justice	10
IV-Surgeon's Involvment	15
V-Jessica's Nightmare	19
VI-The Romance and Horror	23
VII-Dravin's find and his intiative	27
VIII-The attendance to mystery	34
IX-Dravin! the King	40
X-Nihal?	46
XI-Kingdom of Champa	52
XII-The end	59

Conclusion	(xiii)
Postscript	(xv)
Afterword	(xvii)
Epilogue	(xix)
Glossary	(xxi)

Authors Note

This story has been a journey of ideas, effort, and teamwork. First of all this story idea started in my 7th Grade, but eventually in my 9th Grade I decided to publish, I had sprinkled my all essence and ideas in this story, I worked for it like I can, I put all my efforts, I want to make all book readers from children to adults and make them interested in book readings of these types of books namely; science fiction, fantasy, action, mystery, adventure, thriller, mythology, supernatural, drama, and suspense.

This story has many characters Richard, Andrew, Justin, Dr. Ben and his wife and son, Dr. Sen, Jessica, Dravin, Natasha, Mahi, Nihal, 7, 8, Katherine, Kinla, Arnold, and Meriden, this characters and some other side characters had enhanced my story telling.

Acknowledgments

I would like to acknowledge all my friends supporting at starting of the book and my parents until now, even my family, everyone had inspired to deliver this mysterious narrative. They motivated me more to deliver the mesmerizing; gripping; mysterious story. I would like to thank *NOTION PRESS* for providing platform to publish my book.

Character List

- Richard – A skilled and determined individual who plays a crucial role in uncovering hidden truths and ensuring justice. Sharp-minded and always prepared for challenges.

- Andrew – A trusted ally and strong-willed fighter who supports the group during difficult times and plays a key role in strategic planning.

- Justin – A descendant of the powerful Radin family, whose ancestry is deeply connected to the legendary Meriden Sword. He becomes a key figure in the battle between good and evil.

- Dr. Ben – A knowledgeable scientist devoted to research and innovation. His discoveries contribute significantly to the unfolding mystery.

- Dr. Ben's Wife and Son – Important figures in his life who provide emotional support and motivation during difficult times.

- Dr. Sen – Another expert in the field of science, his research and findings influence the events of the story.

- Jessica – A strong and intelligent character who plays a vital role in the team's mission, offering valuable insights and strategies.

- Dravin – A key leader who takes charge of critical situations. He has exceptional combat skills and a deep understanding of strategies, making him an essential part of the conflict.

- Natasha – A sharp and resourceful individual who assists Dravin in leading operations and making crucial decisions during critical moments.

- Mahi – A mysterious and unpredictable character whose true nature is revealed as the story unfolds. Plays an essential role in key events.

- Nihal – A major antagonist who possesses immense power. His connection to the Meriden Sword makes him dangerous, and his rivalry with Dravin leads to an intense battle.

- 7 & 8 – Enigmatic figures whose identities and roles remain crucial to the story's deeper mysteries.

- Katherine – A knowledgeable and observant character who provides important historical insights that help in uncovering hidden secrets.

- Kinla – A strong and tactical individual who supports the team with her intelligence and combat abilities.

- Arnold – A fierce warrior who plays an important role in major battles, using his skills to assist the team.

- Meriden – The legendary ruler of the Champa Empire, who originally wielded the Meriden Sword. His legacy influences the events of the present, making him a key historical figure.

Preface

What started as a simple idea in my 7th-grade notebooks turned into an adventure spanning four years of writing, revising, and reimagining. When my friends initially saw writing as a casual pastime, I, along with my friend Arushh Chakravarthy Tiramdas, saw it as something more—a vision, a world waiting to be built. While others joked about stories, we crafted them. While they treated it as a fleeting amusement, we shaped an entire universe.

Reckoning with the Vector Axe is not just a book; it is the culmination of years of imagination, persistence, and an undying love for storytelling. It is a tale of ancient warriors, forgotten kingdoms, and weapons of unimaginable power—stories that blend reality with myth, battles with emotions, and destiny with choice.

The earliest drafts of this book were very different from what you are about to read. Initially, the story took a different route, with varied characters and alternate settings. Over time, it evolved—shaped by new ideas, expanded with deeper conflicts, and refined to create an immersive experience. The process of revising and perfecting the narrative was as thrilling as the story itself.

At the heart of this book lies the Vector Axe, a weapon of extraordinary power that could change the fate of the world. The story revolves around warriors, rulers, and seekers who are drawn into its mystery—each with their own desires, each with their own battles to fight.

We explore the ancient Kingdom of Champa, a land rich in history, where power struggles and long-buried secrets unfold. Warriors like Richard, Andrew, and Justin step into their destinies, while figures like Dr. Ben, Dr. Sen, and Jessica hold knowledge that could tip the balance between survival and destruction. As the story progresses, the line between friend and foe blurs, and choices determine the fate of entire civilizations.

This book is a journey through time, war, and destiny—where the past whispers into the present, and the echoes of ancient battles refuse to fade.

This book is more than just a fantasy story—it is a piece of my journey, my passion, and my dedication. I hope you enjoy the twists, the battles, and the legends as much as I enjoyed creating them.

To every reader who picks up this book—thank you for stepping into this world. I invite you to explore the Kingdom of Champa, to wield the Vector Axe, and to uncover the truths hidden within the shadows of history.

Enjoy the adventure.

I

The Boy's Past

*

Once upon a time, there lived a young boy who loved playing cricket with his friends every day. He resided in an orphanage alongside his older brother, who was two years his senior. At just four years old, the boy was reluctant to attend school and persistently refused to go, despite being forced.

One day, the orphanage owner asked him, "Why don't you go to school?"

The boy replied, "I don't like it—it's boring."

The owner, trying to advise him like a parent, said, "If you don't go to school, your life will turn out like mine."

Still defiant, the boy pleaded, "I don't want to go! Please don't ask me again."

Curious, the orphanage owner asked, "What are you interested in then?"

Without hesitation, the boy answered, "I love playing cricket."

Understanding the boy's passion, the owner permitted him to play daily with his brother.

One afternoon, while playing, the boy accidentally hit a cricket ball toward a stranger. Enraged, the man approached aggressively, attempting to strike the child. In an effort to defend himself, the boy dodged, and the attacker ended up injuring himself instead. Shaken by the incident, the boy abruptly quit playing cricket and decided to focus on his studies. However, his brother remained adamant and continued to skip school.

Years passed, and the boy studied diligently, eventually securing an impressive rank in his 10th-grade examinations. When the orphanage owner learned of his achievement, he said, "I know how hard you've worked day and night to reach this position."

Grateful, the boy responded, "Everything you did for me was invaluable. Thank you so much."

Smiling, the orphanage owner patted his back and said, "It was your determination that shaped your future, not me."

A decade after the unfortunate cricket incident, the boy finally picked up his bat once more. In his first game back, he played exceptionally well. However, after several matches, he suffered an injury. His brother, concerned for his safety, urged him to be more careful.

The following day, while playing, the boy accidentally struck the ball toward a young man who appeared to be a college student. Infuriated, the man glared at the boy and approached menacingly. Frightened, the boy instinctively tried to evade him but ended up falling and injuring himself. As the man drew closer, his frustration evident, he struck the boy viciously on the head, causing him to faint.

Rushed to the hospital, the boy was admitted to the ICU due to the severity of his injuries. The doctors informed the orphanage owner that the boy had suffered repeated blows to the head and would require at least two weeks to recover.

After the two weeks passed, the orphanage owner was called to the hospital. Though Dravin, the boy's brother, wished to accompany him, the owner refused. Upon arrival, the doctor delivered unexpected news: the boy had lost his memory. However, he kept repeating the name "Dravin."

Realizing that he was attempting to recall his brother, the orphanage owner called for Dravin. When Dravin arrived at the hospital and saw his brother's condition, he immediately tested his memory by asking an educational question. The boy answered correctly, proving that he still retained his knowledge. However, the orphanage owner mistakenly believed that he was no longer important to the boy.

One day, while walking with his brother, the boy tried to piece together fragments of his past. Suddenly, they witnessed a similar incident—someone being hit by a cricket ball and fainting. Seeing this, the boy collapsed, unconscious. When he woke up six to seven hours later, he was shocked to find that his memories had fully returned.

Determined to build a successful future, he resumed his studies with renewed vigor. Years of hard work eventually paid off, and he secured a well-paying job. Despite being financially capable of purchasing his own home, he chose to remain in the orphanage. Out of gratitude, he donated 60% of his salary to the institution that had raised him, living a content and fulfilling life.

II

Andrew is attacked

A boy named Andrew was born into a wealthy family in Shinephill. From the moment of his birth, his parents believed that their fortune had doubled and considered him a symbol of prosperity. His upbringing was meticulously guided by his parents, and he followed their teachings diligently. Excelling in his studies, he secured the highest marks in the state for his 10th-grade exams and was consistently praised by his teachers. Throughout his journey, he always held onto his mother's motivational words, which fueled his determination. With a peaceful life and remarkable academic achievements, he made his parents proud.

Upon joining college, Andrew encountered a notorious group known as the Ballais gang. One of the members frequently requested him to complete their records, and though he complied initially, the workload steadily increased. Over time, Andrew began refusing their demands, unwilling to let them interfere with his studies. Three months later, he developed feelings for a girl named Veresicca and eventually confessed his love to her. However, she remained undecided, neither accepting nor rejecting his feelings. Around the same time, Ballais approached Andrew and revealed, "I've had feelings for Veresicca for the past year. I don't care if she dates you or not, but I have already expressed my love to her."

Annoyed, Andrew retorted, "First, you should focus on your studies before worrying about relationships." Ballais, unbothered by Andrew's words, dismissed his remark.

Days later, Ballais began coercing Veresicca into accepting his love, disregarding her feelings entirely. His persistence crossed the line, and in frustration, Veresicca slapped him. Enraged, Ballais retaliated violently, smashing her head against a wall, rendering her unconscious. Tragically, she succumbed to a brain hemorrhage and a severe concussion. When Andrew discovered her fate, he was devastated and directly confronted Ballais. Their argument escalated into a physical altercation. As the fight progressed, Ballais struggled to retaliate, prompting his entire gang to intervene. They viciously attacked Andrew, leaving his face severely disfigured. Staggering from his injuries, Andrew began making his way home.

While walking, he was unexpectedly struck by a cricket ball. Glancing at the boy responsible, he approached him and, in a fit of rage, repeatedly struck the boy's head with a rock before continuing his journey. Upon reaching home, he was met with an unexpected surprise—his cousins had gathered to celebrate with him. However, the moment he stepped inside, the entire room erupted in screams. His parents, horrified by his appearance, reacted with shock and distress. Without delay, they rushed him to the hospital.

Upon arrival, the doctors immediately admitted him to the ICU. His wounds were cleaned, and after a day of careful observation, the doctors informed his parents that the injuries had permanently altered his facial structure.

A surgical procedure was performed, restoring his appearance to its original state. With his face healed, Andrew resumed his life, carrying the weight of his past experiences with him.

III

Devotes Justice

A boy named Justin was born into an orthodox Brahmin family. Though he was not born in his native country, he pursued his education in India. He studied at a traditional Indian school called Gurukul, where he spent ten years without meeting his parents. During his time there, he excelled in his studies, remained devoted to prayer, and lived a disciplined life, becoming deeply devoted to God. Upon completing his education, he returned to his native country and established his own industry.

As he worked towards success, Justin encountered numerous challenges and faced many who envied his progress. When he finally reached a competitive level, most adversaries reconciled with him—except for a man named Arnold. Arnold's industry was located right next to Justin's, making them direct neighbors. Initially, Arnold claimed his factory specialized in manufacturing flour, but in reality, he was producing and distributing drugs. Despite multiple government raids, no evidence of illegal activity was found. However, Justin knew the truth, as Arnold had admitted his crimes in a fit of rage. Furthermore, Justin was aware that Arnold's factory was releasing harmful chemicals, severely affecting the environment. Leveraging his influence, Justin ensured the central government conducted another raid, during which Arnold was caught red-handed. Consequently, Arnold's factory was seized, fueling his resentment toward Justin. Seeking revenge, Arnold devised a plan to kill him.

With the help of a detective, Arnold meticulously plotted his attack. The day arrived for him to execute his plan. Through surveillance, he learned that Justin meditated daily in front of God, remaining still for long periods, unaware of his surroundings. Arnold and his skilled accomplices infiltrated Justin's home. Upon entering, they saw Justin's father watching television. Without hesitation, Arnold beheaded him. They looted Justin's wealth and fled, unaware that the house had CCTV surveillance.

Emerging from meditation, Justin heard noises and descended the stairs, only to find his father's lifeless body. Overcome with shock, he rushed to the CCTV surveillance room, where he discovered that Arnold and his gang were responsible for his father's murder and theft. Filled with anguish, Justin retreated to the prayer room and meditated with deep concentration, seeking divine intervention. His devotion was so profound that God was pleased.

Then God appeared before him and asked, "मह्यां प्रति भवतः सर्वेभ्यः प्रार्थनानां कृते अहं अतीव कृतज्ञः अस्मि, भवतां प्रार्थनां दत्त्वा पुनः धन्यवादं ददामि, भवन्तं किम् अपेक्षितम्?" (Translation: I am very thankful for all your prayers towards me. I would thank you back by granting you a wish. What do you want?)

Justin replied, "भगवतः, यः मम पितरं हतवान् तस्य वधाय शस्त्रम् आवश्यकम्।" (Translation: God, I need a weapon to slay the person who killed my father.)

God responded, "अयमेव, अहं भवतः कृते एकं अक्षं समर्पयिष्यामि यत् मम पक्षतः उपहारः अस्ति।" (Translation: Okay, I will hand over an axe to you that is a gift from my side.)

God then plucked a leaf from the universe tree and summoned all the gods to sacrifice a drop of blood on a piece of metal. He then took a cotton cloth and inscribed the rules for using the divine axe:

१. इति। यदि कश्चित् व्यक्तिः एतं अक्षं उपयोक्तुम् इच्छति, प्रथमं अहं स्वीकर्तुम् इच्छामि, यदि अहं स्वीकरोमि, यदा कश्चित् एतत् अक्षं प्राप्स्यति तदा ते आत्मानं वा अन्यान् वा म्रियितुं तस्य उपयोगं कुर्युः।

२. इति। यदि कश्चित् व्यक्तिः एकस्य उपयोगं करोति, तर्हि ते कस्मिंश्चित् रोगेण वा कस्मिंश्चित् शस्त्रैः वा मारिताः भविष्यन्ति, सिवायं एतत् अक्षं निगूढरूपेण।

(Translation:

1.   If any person wants to use this axe, first I must accept. If I accept, whenever someone receives this axe, they must use it to kill either themselves or another.

2.   If any person uses it once, they will mysteriously die from an illness or weapon, except for this axe.)

Without hesitation, Justin went to Arnold's office and instantly beheaded him. However, as per the divine rule, Justin suffered a fatal heart attack. Before his death, he married a woman named Kimla, ensuring that his family lineage continued into future generations.

✝14✝

IV

Surgeon's involvement

✳

Once upon a time, there lived a doctor named Ben, a junior doctor with a dream of becoming a senior surgeon. He worked tirelessly, passing his junior level, completing one hundred self-tests, and enduring six-hour exams, ultimately achieving his goal in fifteen years. He had a small family consisting of his wife and their nine-year-old son. Dr. Ben was a patient and understanding father, not even reacting when his son scored 6/20 in math.

One weekend, he decided to spend time with his family at a mall. As they set off on their journey, they found themselves driving alongside a large convoy. Dr. Ben's son eagerly asked him to overtake the convoy, and as he did, their vehicle suddenly broke down, as did the vehicle behind them. Dr. Ben tried restarting the car, but it wouldn't budge, and the same issue affected the convoy vehicle.

A man from the convoy approached and said, "Our vehicle has finally started, but we don't know how long it will last."

Dr. Ben replied, "I think it's because my son asked me to overtake, and ever since then, both vehicles stopped."

Suddenly, the police arrived and arrested the man who was speaking with Dr. Ben. As they inspected the convoy, they discovered drugs hidden in packets inside rice bags. The police intelligence department had been tracking the smugglers, and thanks to the incident, they were able to apprehend them. Realizing the danger of the situation, Dr. Ben quickly closed the windows and drove away as the bystanders stared at his son.

One morning, Dr. Ben informed his child that he wouldn't be home that night and asked him to stay safe. Later, he dropped his son off at school. After school, his son returned home safely by bus, freshened up, ate some snacks, and went out to play with his friends. At Dr. Ben's request, his wife accompanied their son to the playground.

While playing, a man—the same one who had been caught smuggling drugs because of Dr. Ben's son—approached him. Suddenly, a flaming axe appeared mysteriously in the man's hands, and he struck the child fiercely. Dr. Ben's wife had stepped away to use the restroom, and when she returned, she was horrified to see her son fatally wounded. She immediately called Dr. Ben, who had just completed a successful surgery. Before he could process the news, his wife screamed in agony, revealing that their son had died.

Dr. Ben instructed his wife to bring their son to the hospital immediately. With the help of a driver, she rushed there, and the child was taken straight to the ICU. As a patient exited the ICU and Dr. Ben's child was wheeled inside, Dr. Ben's wife suddenly let out a terrified scream.

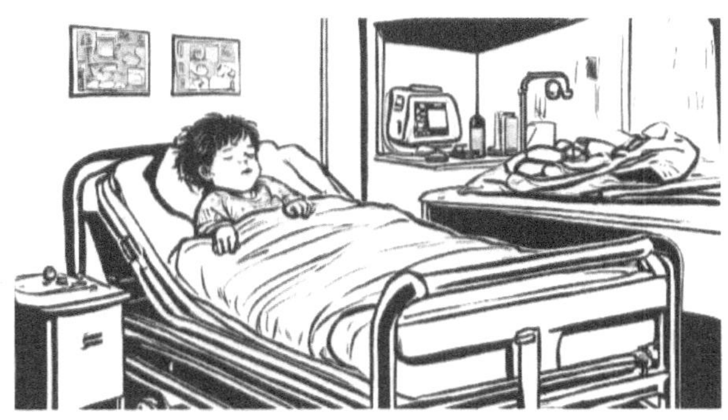

Dr. Ben, alarmed, asked, "Why did you scream?"
With a trembling voice, his wife replied, "H-He is the one who killed our son."

Dr. Ben turned to confirm, "Are you absolutely sure this is the man?"

"Yes, I am certain," she answered.

A fellow doctor soon approached Dr. Ben with devastating news—his son had succumbed to his injuries. The loss took a toll on Dr. Ben's mental health, and despite his attempts to cope, his condition only worsened, especially after the passing of his brother, Sen, who was also a doctor. However, over time, he slowly recovered and began researching the Vector—the mysterious axe that had played a role in his son's death.

V

Jessica's Nightmare

Jessica was born into a poor family and had a good childhood, though she never formally studied because of her parents' financial struggles. Her mother worked in a school, and Jessica would stand near the window, secretly listening to lessons. She had immense potential, and the school principal noticed her. Every day, he called Jessica to clarify her doubts, eventually paying for her education. Through sheer determination, she studied hard, pursued nursing, and became a nurse after four years. She had always dreamed of this career, as it was her mother's wish for her. The principal, where her mother worked, praised her success.

"Very good! You have succeeded and honored my kindness. May you be blessed with more luck!" he said.

Jessica continued working diligently, eventually becoming the head nurse. Doctors recommended her for the position, recognizing her talent and dedication. One day, she assisted Dr. Sen, the brother of Dr. Ben, in a critical surgery. The patient was a gangster, and Dr. Sen alerted everyone to proceed cautiously. However, during the operation, the patient's pulse suddenly dropped, and he died of a heart attack. Dr. Sen asked Jessica to inform the family.

Jessica stepped out and solemnly said, "I'm sorry to inform you, but despite our best efforts, we were unable to save him."

The gangster's child, devastated, demanded to see the doctor. Jessica led him to Dr. Sen's office and left. Inside, the child, filled with rage, asked, "Why didn't you save my father?"

Dr. Sen mockingly replied, "It was out of my hands."

The boy, overcome with fury, suddenly summoned a flaming axe and struck Dr. Sen, killing him instantly. Jessica, arriving to call Dr. Sen for a check-up, witnessed the murder and ran for her life.

At home, she was drenched in sweat. Her mother, alarmed, asked, "What happened? Why do you look so tense?"

Jessica, still in shock, stammered, "I saw Dr. Sen get murdered… by a child wielding a flaming axe."

Her mother immediately called the police. The child was about to be arrested when he suddenly vomited blood and died. Jessica, shaken, decided to research the mysterious axe. She moved to Petrogeme, where she visited the market daily, always ending her trip at a library. One day, she noticed a man engrossed in a book about vector axes. Curious, she approached and asked, "Who are you, and why are you researching the axe?"

"I'm Dr. Ben," the man replied. "My child and my brother were both killed by this mysterious axe. I'm trying to understand it."

Jessica's eyes widened. "Your brother… is he Dr. Sen? You look just like him! I worked with him."

Dr. Ben nodded. "Yes! How do you know my brother?"

Jessica explained her connection, and Dr. Ben asked, "Would you be interested in collaborating with me?"

"Yes," she agreed without hesitation.

Their conversation was overheard by a man named Richard, who stepped forward. "I want to join as well."

Jessica eyed him warily. "Who are you?"

"I'm Richard. I live with two roommates, Flamine and Carie. I wanted them to join me in researching this axe, but they refused. I lost my memory once, but one day, while walking with my brother Dravin, a sound triggered my past. I've faced tragedies… I was attacked twice just for accidentally hitting strangers with a cricket ball."

Jessica and Dr. Ben listened, intrigued. However, tragedy struck when Dr. Ben and Richard died in an accident while heading to Jessica's ancestral house.

VI

The Romance and Horror

Jessica, after enduring numerous tragedies, decided to take a trip to clear her mind. She traveled to the peaceful town of Shinephill, where she encountered Katherine, the mother of Flamine and Carie. Katherine, sensing Jessica's distress, urged her to prioritize her safety and seek a tranquil life before departing.

As Jessica explored the town, she saw a man and instantly felt a deep connection. That evening, she learned that he was staying at the same resort. Unable to contain her emotions, she proposed to him within three days. Fate was in her favor, as he too had fallen in love at first sight. "I am Andrew," he introduced himself. "My face appears this way because I underwent surgery. My past was far from pleasant."

As time passed, they grew to understand each other, and after two years, they were happily married with the blessing of both families.

Jessica continued her research on the mysterious axe upon returning home. Her mother, sensing Jessica's determination, gifted her a book written by Jessica's grandfather. This book, titled Vector Axe Chronicles, contained detailed accounts of the legendary vector axe. As she immersed herself in its pages, she uncovered a shocking revelation—the axe's power was initially restricted, but due to certain individuals' desires and actions, it had acquired an extended, almost unstoppable force.

Driven by curiosity, Jessica decided to investigate further by visiting her ancestral home. Upon arrival, she discovered an old bunker, hidden beneath the house. Inside, she found a board displaying a list of names— those fated to die at the hands of the vector axe.

Jessica hesitated before reading the names. But the moment she laid eyes on them, a wave of horror struck her. Within four days, Jessica tragically passed away.

Her death was orchestrated by Justin's grandson, who, due to long-standing family conflicts with Arnold's son, manipulated the divine rules governing the vector axe. He successfully convinced the higher powers to alter fate—anyone attempting to research the axe would perish within four days. This change took effect immediately upon his request.

The names on the board were:

ARNOLD, DR.SEN, DR.BEN, JESSICA, RICHARD, KATHERINE, KINLA.

In the heavens, a voice resonated through the cosmic realm.

"वेक्टर्-अक्षैः संबद्धाः जनाः मृताः, इदानीं अहं अस्मिन् जगत्यां अवसरं ददामि यत्र अहं पुरातनानां प्रति नियमानं परिवर्त्य मम पुत्रं अधः वृष्टवान्, द्राविन् एन्डू तथा रिचर्ड इत्येतयोः व्यक्तिगत-दिनचर्याम् पठितुम् आरब्धवान्।"

(Translation: The people connected to the vector axe have perished. Now, I grant this world a chance, restoring the ancient rules. My son Dravin now reads through Andrew's and Richard's personal diaries.)

VII

Dravin's find and his initiative

Dravin, after reading Andrew and Richard's diaries, was deeply shaken. The revelations in Richard's diary, in particular, left him in utter disbelief. As he delved deeper into their pasts, Dravin found himself entangled in a journey that led him to discover unexpected truths about his own life. Amidst this journey, he met Natasha, a woman he had loved for the past five years.

One day, Dravin approached the orphanage owner, who had raised him, and said, "I have been in love with Natasha for five years. Can I marry her?"

The orphanage owner replied, "It's your life and your choice, but I must advise you—do not marry someone you will regret in the future."

Dravin, determined, went with the orphanage owner to Natasha's home to formally propose their marriage to her parents. With Natasha's insistence, her parents agreed, and the two were happily married.

On the night of his wedding, Dravin received an urgent call from the orphanage owner, requesting his presence. Curious and slightly anxious, Dravin rushed to the orphanage, where he was immediately directed to the office. As soon as he stepped in, the orphanage owner exclaimed, "My son, you have finally learned the truth about your life. Do not be shocked."

Dravin, bewildered, replied, "What are you talking about?!"

With a deep sigh, the orphanage owner said, "Dravin, your parents had a love marriage just like you and Natasha. They left you in my care because they were threatened by someone who forbade them from keeping you. I was their trusted friend and took you in as part of my orphanage. Your parents loved you deeply but had no choice. They asked me to reveal the truth only after you were married."

Tears streamed down Dravin's face. He was overwhelmed with happiness upon learning about his parents but also saddened by the hardships they had endured. The orphanage owner then showed him old photographs of his childhood with his parents. Dravin stared at them in silence before abruptly leaving.

As he walked away, the orphanage owner called out, "There is one more thing you need to know!"

Dravin, still emotional, responded, "Later!" and hurried off.

The following day, unable to shake his curiosity, he called the orphanage owner and asked, "You had something important to tell me yesterday, right? What is it?"

With a solemn voice, the orphanage owner replied, "Brace yourself. Your parents were murdered. They were forced to drink sulfuric acid."

Dravin, shocked beyond words, immediately hung up the phone and fell into a deep silence for two months.

Eventually, he began to recover and decided to take action. He formulated a plan to establish an organization called "Vector Axe Intelligence" (VAI) to investigate and address the mysteries surrounding the Vector Axe. He formally submitted an application to the government:

Dravin Ron Millets

St. No.: 21, Ward No.: 17/2

Kansas City, Missouri, 64112

dravin@yahoo.com

+1 816 913 385356

19/08/1991

Ame Govert

2201 C St., NW

Washington, DC 20520

Subject: Application for Approval and Recognition of Vector Axe Intelligence (VAI)

Dear Ame Govert,

I trust this letter finds you well. My name is Dravin Ron Millets, and I am writing to formally apply for the approval and recognition of Vector Axe Intelligence (VAI), an organization dedicated to investigating and addressing incidents related to the mysterious Vector Axe.

I. Purpose and Objectives:

● Conducting comprehensive research on Vector Axe incidents to unravel its origins, powers, and potential dangers.

● Collaborating with experts, researchers, and government agencies to enhance our collective understanding of the Vector Axe phenomenon.

● Providing support in investigating and documenting Vector Axe cases to contribute to public safety.

II. Structure and Functionality: Executive Team:

● President: Dravin Ron Millets

● Vice President: Natasha Dravin Ron Millets

● Research Director: Katherine Venny Scotten

● Operations Director: To be appointed by the government

Research Division:

● Conducting in-depth studies on Vector Axe-related incidents.

● Engaging in collaborative research initiatives with external experts.

Operations Division:

● Responding to Vector Axe incidents in coordination with law enforcement.

● Ensuring the safety and protection of affected individuals.

Public Awareness and Outreach:

● Disseminating information about Vector Axe incidents to the public.

- Conducting educational programs to raise awareness.

III. Resources and Funding:

- Seeking funding through government grants and private donations.

- Allocating funds for research, operations, and public awareness campaigns.

IV. Collaboration with Government Agencies:

- Commitment to collaborating with law enforcement agencies, sharing information, and providing support in Vector Axe-related cases.

- Requesting government support for research initiatives and access to relevant data.

V. Accountability and Reporting:

- Providing regular reports to the government department overseeing VAI's activities.

- Maintaining transparency in operations and adhering to ethical standards.

I kindly request a meeting to discuss this application further and address any inquiries. I firmly believe that Vector Axe Intelligence can significantly contribute to understanding and mitigating the impact of Vector Axe incidents.

Thank you for considering this application, and I look forward to the opportunity to contribute to the safety and well-being of our community.

Sincerely,
Dravin Ron Millets
Dravin R. M.

After a series of discussions, the government approved the proposal, and VAI was officially launched. Dravin was elated to see his vision come to life, but just as he began to enjoy his success, two young children suddenly appeared from nowhere.

VIII

The attendance to mystery

The classroom was buzzing with noise when the teacher called out, "Nihal Sanshetti... Nihal Sanshetti... Nihaal?"

There was no response. His friend nudged him, bringing him back to reality, and Nihal finally muttered, "Present."

The whole class burst into laughter. "Are you deaf?" someone yelled. Nihal shot them a sharp glare, and silence fell over the room.

Concerned, the teacher turned to Nihal's friend, Mahi Sheelki. "What's wrong with him?"

Mahi hesitated before replying, "Sir, it's a long story. If you meet me in the canteen during milk time, I'll tell you everything."

That evening, as planned, the teacher met Mahi. "Now tell me," the teacher said. "What's going on with Nihal?"

Mahi took a deep breath. "Sir, it's a long story. Sit back— it'll take a while."

The teacher nodded. "Alright, go ahead."

Mahi began, "Nihal Sanshetti was born in a small town in Indonesia, formerly the Kingdom of Champa. His childhood was both a blessing and a struggle. He lived in a joint family with six identical houses built side by side. Even before he was born, his mother had a near-death experience while climbing an unfinished staircase. Luckily, she survived, and soon after, Nihal was born."

He continued, "From an early age, Nihal was very attached to his father. He would always run to him with complaints, like a little child seeking comfort. However, his childhood was not free of troubles. He developed an addiction to video games, which his sister scolded him harshly for. From that day on, he stopped playing. His cousins, who were three to four years older, often excluded him from trips and outings, making him feel left out."

"Then came the pandemic. In fifth grade, Nihal and his family contracted COVID-19. During their time in quarantine, they grew closer, but there was always one problem—his parents constantly fought. One day, his mother, overwhelmed by stress, attempted to end her life by drowning in a lake. She turned off her phone and walked away, but at the last moment, she stopped herself. That day, Nihal saw his father cry for the first time. When his mother returned, he hugged her tightly and begged her never to leave him again."

Mahi sighed before continuing, "During a summer break, Nihal's mother took him and his sister to stay at her sister's house. There, he overheard his mother refusing to return home, stating that she wanted to stay there permanently. When his father arrived, he gave Nihal an ultimatum: either stay with him or with his mother. There was no real choice—they had to leave with their father. However, soon after, his parents had a heated argument with their relatives. Eventually, they reconciled, and their fights ceased. Life seemed to return to normal."

"But despite all this, Nihal rarely stayed with his parents. He lived with his grandmother in the house next door, spending most of his time with her. He even moved some of his clothes there. He misses her terribly now."

The teacher sat in stunned silence. "For now, that's enough. Let's continue tomorrow at dinner."

The next day, an emergency announcement echoed through the school. "Nihal... our student... is flying in the sky!"

Students and teachers rushed to the scene, only to see a glowing diamond embed itself in Nihal's chest. Panicked, everyone ran—including Mahi.

That night, when things settled, Nihal was nowhere to be found. Search teams combed through every corner of the school for three weeks, but no trace of him remained. Since Nihal was from an orphanage, there wasn't much concern. Life moved on.

A year later, the teacher found Mahi in the canteen and asked, "Shall we continue?"

Mahi nodded. "Yes, let's continue. After the pandemic, Nihal's father planned to send him to a hostel. He was supposed to go to another school first, but due to COVID, he ended up here in seventh grade. He struggled with academics, new people, and a different environment. He missed his parents terribly and often cried. Over time, he adjusted but faced bullying. By eighth grade, he had

earned the favor of his Hindi, Social Studies, and Computer teachers. He helped others during exams but was falsely accused of using people. After that, he withdrew socially but continued assisting his classmates."
Mahi's expression darkened. "Then came the biggest change. Nihal began behaving strangely. He stopped responding to people but was affectionate towards his family. Eventually, he fell into deep depression. He developed suicidal thoughts—13 times in two years. After joining this school, he improved. His mental health stabilized, he gained control over his emotions, and he matured. Then, he fell in love. He confessed to a girl named Vekris, but she kept him waiting for a year with no reply. His friends bullied him over it."
Mahi clenched his fists. "His mental health spiraled again. He went through cycles of recovery and relapse 15 times. Even after disappearing, I can't shake the feeling that there's a mystery behind all this."
The teacher stood up, saluted Mahi, and said, "You people are complex. Why do you overthink so much? Be careful, okay?"
Twelve years passed. Nihal was still missing. One day, someone found his old watch. Excited, they showed it to

Nihal's former roommate, who remarked, "Oh, he threw that away in anger once."

They searched again, but no clues were found. Nihal remained lost in time, a mystery unsolved.
And Mahi? He still missed him.

IX
Dravin! the King

One day, after VAI had completed their meeting, Dravin was seen unusually happy. Suddenly, two young kids materialized in front of him out of nowhere, facing the chaos around them. Shocked, Dravin immediately asked, "Who are you two?"

One of the kids stepped forward and said, "I am Akshin." The other followed, "I am Akshiy. You can call us 7 and 8, respectively."

Dravin, still trying to process the situation, asked, "Where are you from?"

7 replied, "We are from Gladstone. You know, the town beside Kansas."

"Okay... but why are you here?" Dravin questioned.

8 responded, "We teleported here using VAS—the Vector Axe Stone. We recently lost our parents, and we came to you because of what we know about Vector Axe."

Dravin's eyes widened in shock. "VAS? How did you even get that?"

7 explained, "Our uncle Justin gave it to us. After getting married, it took him two years to return home, and then he entrusted it to us."

Dravin's mind raced. "How come he never mentioned this in his personal diary?" he thought.

Seeing their pleading eyes, 7 and 8 asked together, "Dravin, sir, can we stay with you? Our uncle Justin told us about you. Please!"

After a brief pause, Dravin sighed and said, "Okay."

They started living together, with 7 and 8 rejoining their old school, learning more about Vector Axe, and enjoying life. One day, while teaching them about Vector Axe, Dravin asked, "Where is VAS now? Do you still have it?"

7 shook his head. "No, it suddenly disappeared."

Dravin paused, then said, "Alright," and continued the lesson.

Ten years later, the two had grown into well-educated young adults. One day, a stranger arrived and introduced himself. "Hey! I'm Mahi. I believe you guys can help me find my friend."

7 nodded. "Okay. How can we help?"

Mahi responded, "Let me tell Dravin the whole story first." He narrated the mysterious disappearance of his friend Nihal and then left. When 7 and 8 returned home and relayed the story, Dravin was shocked. He had a gut feeling that this tale would be crucial someday. The next day, he shared the story with the entire office, leaving everyone stunned. Some even speculated that the events were linked to Vector Axe (VA).

One day, 7 and 8 remembered something their uncle Justin had once told them:

"Give this to Dravin. With this, he must rule the world."

That day, their uncle had handed them a ring.

They approached Dravin and asked him to wear it, explaining what Justin had said. The moment Dravin put on the ring, an immense surge of strength coursed through him. A mysterious mark appeared on his right hand, reading: "THE KING OF VECTOR AXE."

Realizing his newfound abilities, Dravin discovered he could sense past and future murders. Stunned, he gathered his team and shared the revelation. During the discussion, a colleague theorized:

"I think 7 and 8 are deeply connected to VA. Not that they're in danger, but rather, everything happening around them seems tied to VA. They are the starting point of these strange events. We should observe them carefully."

Dravin fell into deep thought and began dedicating three hours daily to studying 7 and 8, searching for hidden clues.

Strangely, 7 and 8 started vanishing from home at odd times. Natasha frequently called Dravin, reporting, "They left suddenly again."

Yet, every time Dravin rushed home, they would already be back. Suspicious, Dravin confronted them one day.

"Are you working for someone? You're acting mysteriously."

7 sighed and replied, "You overthink too much. We visit Justin's funeral every day. He asked us to behave this way. We don't know more about VA than you do—you taught us! We promise we will never betray you."

To prove their sincerity, they placed their hands on Dravin's head, assuring him of their loyalty. Relieved, Dravin shared this with the team, and everyone continued their normal duties.

One day, all VAI systems simultaneously glitched, but since nothing seemed amiss, no one reported it. However, moments later, a chilling message appeared on every screen:

"YOU WILL BE IN DANGER SOON, DRAVIN! I WILL SEE YOU. I WILL TAKE GOOD CARE OF YOU. BE READY FOR THE ULTIMATE BATTLE, WHICH MAY DESTROY THIS WORLD."

Panic spread through the organization. Dravin was immediately called in. He stared at the message, his mind racing. Without hesitation, he summoned an emergency meeting.

In the meeting, he issued strict safety protocols and assigned tasks to his team. He gathered his most trusted members and warned them:

"If anything feels suspicious, inform me immediately. If you suspect anyone or have doubts, speak up. This is serious."

With the weight of an impending catastrophe looming over them, everyone dispersed, resuming their duties with newfound vigilance.

X

Nihal??

Mahi was roaming around with a teacher named Sathya, who had previously listened to the story of Nihal. Everything seemed fine as they walked together, but suddenly, out of nowhere, Nihal appeared from behind and hugged Mahi. Shocked beyond words, Mahi realized he was seeing Nihal after fifteen years. Overwhelmed with emotions, he immediately began asking about Nihal's well-being.

"Where were you all these years? Why did you disappear? And how did you get back?" Mahi questioned eagerly.

But just then, Mahi jolted awake. It was a dream.

He splashed water on his face, trying to shake off the surreal experience. That evening, he went to a café to clear his mind. As he sat down, a man approached him abruptly, struck him hard, and ran away before anyone could react. Mahi couldn't see who it was.

Moments later, another person sat beside him and began speaking.

"I was trapped in a place called VAT—Vector Axe Trap. I saw everything happening around me, I heard things, I felt things. They told me I was stuck there because a stone called VAS—Vector Axe Stone—somehow entered my chest. It took me ten years to separate from it, and they made me stay for an additional five years. It seems that whenever VAS is used for teleportation, someone else gets randomly trapped in VAT. It was my fate. But now, I'm back. Don't worry, I have more responsibilities now, and I need to take care of things. I'll stay with you—you don't have to worry anymore."

Mahi stared at him, realization hitting him like a storm. It was Nihal. Without hesitation, he hugged him tightly, tears streaming down his face. They talked for hours, catching up. Mahi recounted everything that had happened before Nihal's return, and to his surprise, Nihal chuckled and said,

"That was me, you fool! I forgot I had powers and accidentally hit you. My bad!"

Mahi shook his head and laughed. "No problem, man."

The next day, Nihal decided to visit his old orphanage. He first went to the orphanage's attendant and asked, "How are you, Anna? I was trapped all these years, but I finally made it back. How is Uncle?"

The attendant's expression darkened. "Hey, I'm fine... But your uncle, he passed away."

Nihal was stunned. He collapsed to the ground, crying. Two hours later, he composed himself and accepted the painful truth. He then went to find his childhood friend; Pricen, "How are you? I know things aren't great, but still..." Nihal said softly.

Pricen hugged him tightly, sobbing uncontrollably.

Anger flickered in Nihal's eyes. "Are you crying because Uncle died? You should be happy! We always wished for this, didn't we? He only ever supported Dravin and Justin. He never cared about us. He gave them all the privileges while ignoring us. Be happy!"

Pricen sniffled and said, "No, it's not that… I was happy, but Dravin found out. One day, he came to me, beat me, and tortured me when he learned I was glad about Uncle's death."

Nihal's face darkened. "I'll take care of it. Don't worry."

That evening, Nihal met Mahi and said, "I forgot to mention something. You remember Pricen, right? Back when we were kids, we despised Uncle because he always favored Dravin and Justin over us. He thought we were immature because we kept to ourselves. Once, I hit Justin in the face with a cricket ball, and from that day on, Uncle held a grudge. And now Dravin punished Pricen just for celebrating his death."

Mahi clenched his fists. "I'll help you."

And with that, a sinister plan began to take shape. Mahi, Nihal, and Pricen—pure psychopaths—set their sights on Dravin, the King of VA. Their goal: to eliminate him and destroy the world. They began extensive research on VA, studying its history, strengths, and weaknesses. Eventually, they moved to Kansas, settled in a shared apartment, and continued their research.

They devised a plan for revenge near VAI headquarters. However, realizing a direct attack would be too risky, they instead decided to infiltrate VAI from within. Mahi and Nihal created fake identities—Mahel and Nimel, respectively. They applied for jobs at VAI, and by sheer luck, they passed the selection process and were invited for an interview with Dravin himself.

One by one, they faced Dravin. Both managed to impress him and secured positions within VAI. Over time, through dedication and intelligence, they climbed the ranks. As trust in them grew, even Dravin himself began to see them as valuable employees.

But behind the scenes, they were slowly breaking the system.

They learned more about Dravin, Natasha, and even 7 and 8. One fateful night, they sneaked into Dravin's office to steal classified documents. Just as they were about to escape, the door suddenly creaked open. Dravin entered the room.

Heart pounding, they pressed themselves against the wall behind a curtain, holding their breath. Dravin scanned the room, seemingly unaware of their presence. After a tense five minutes, he finally left. They had narrowly escaped detection.

Realizing the danger, they decided to lay low for a while, resisting any further suspicious actions... for now.

XI
Kingdom of Champa

"Meriden, Meriden, come here!" The young prince was being called by his father, King Radin of Champa. The kingdom, located in present-day southern Vietnam, flourished under his rule, known for his wisdom, generosity, and unwavering sense of justice. He was beloved by his people and respected by neighboring empires, having forged strong alliances through his kindness and assistance in times of crisis.

One fateful day, an enraged man stormed into the King's Court. Rather than responding with anger, King Radin asked calmly, "Why are you here, my good man? Can you explain?"

The man, still seething, retorted, "You claim to be a just ruler, yet our people are suffering from a severe water crisis while you sit here in luxury! I even informed the Wish Granter, but nothing was done."

King Radin's face darkened, but he maintained his composure. "Calm yourself. I was not informed. This was a grave mistake on the part of the Wish Granter, and for that, I deeply apologize on behalf of the throne."

The Wish Granter was summoned immediately. This time, the King's anger flared, his voice thunderous, "Why did you not inform me of this crisis?"

Trembling, the Wish Granter bowed deeply. "My Lord, I sincerely apologize. My wife was pregnant, and in my distraction, I forgot."

The King's expression softened. "I understand the responsibilities of family, but this negligence cannot happen again. Do you understand?"

"Yes, My Lord!" the Wish Granter replied earnestly.

The man who had initially burst in felt immense relief. "Thank the gods he didn't yell at me like that!" he thought, before bowing and expressing gratitude.

King Radin smiled. "Never stop speaking up when injustice arises. I admire your passion."

Meriden, the prince, watched these interactions with great interest. He idolized his father but disliked his moments of temper. Meriden had been born after a long period without a royal heir. Desperate for a successor, King Radin had sought the wisdom of Saint Lingeshwar, who guided him to perform the sacred 'Garbhadhana Samskara.' Soon after, Queen Radia conceived, and Meriden was born on the auspicious third day of Shukla Paksha, the same day as Lord Parashurama.

From a young age, Meriden exhibited great curiosity and bravery. One day, while playing outside the kingdom with his friends, he noticed a man practicing combat—

shooting arrows, wielding a sword, and displaying incredible battle techniques. Captivated, Meriden secretly observed and practiced the skills he saw.

One evening, he approached his father. "Father, I have been training in archery and combat. Please send me to a Gurukul to study properly."

King Radin chuckled. "Oh, my son, you are only five! I will send you when you turn eight."

Disappointed, Meriden walked away. Later that night, King Radin pondered how to encourage his son. "Perhaps I should train him myself," he mused.

Summoning Meriden, the King began instructing him in the basics. To his astonishment, Meriden demonstrated an advanced understanding of combat. "Where did you learn this?" the King asked, astonished.

Meriden led his father to the mysterious warrior he had been observing. To King Radin's surprise, it was none other than King Rakesh of the Khmer Kingdom, an old friend and one of the greatest warriors of their time.

"Rad! What a surprise!" Rakesh greeted him warmly.

King Radin explained how his son had secretly learned from Rakesh's training sessions and made a bold request. "Will you train my son?"

Rakesh smiled. "Yes, but under strict conditions. He will not see his family for twelve years, and he may return only when I decide."

Radin turned to his son. "What do you say?"

Without hesitation, Meriden declared, "I am ready."

"Not so fast! Spend the next seven days with your family. After that, he is yours to train," Radin insisted.

After a week of farewells, Meriden embarked on his journey. As he entered the training grounds, Rakesh asked, "Do you not miss your family?"

Meriden, with determination in his eyes, replied, "They watch over me from the heavens. I have no need to cry."

For twelve grueling years, Meriden trained under Rakesh's guidance, emerging as a formidable warrior and strategist. When the time came, King Radin organized a grand event to showcase his son's abilities. Archery, sword fighting, hand-to-hand combat—Meriden excelled in all, leaving the spectators in awe.

Following his triumphant return, Meriden was introduced to Ushia, the daughter of King Unia of Silius. The royal families arranged their marriage, which took place on Hanuman Jayanti in a grand celebration uniting the two kingdoms.

Years later, King Radin passed the throne to Meriden, who ruled with the same wisdom and kindness as his father. Under his leadership, the kingdom thrived.

One fateful day, a massive rock hurtled toward Silius and Champa. With no one to stop it, Meriden seized his bow and, invoking a divine mantra, shattered the rock. In recognition of his bravery, his father, Guru Rakesh, and King Unia bestowed upon him a legendary sword forged from the blood of three kings and sacred iron from the three kingdoms.

"Speak the name 'Purushottam' to create laws that none may break," they told him. "If you wield this sword, it must be used for battle, and once drawn, it must taste blood."

Years passed, and Meriden ruled wisely. But even great rulers must eventually depart. At the age of 102, as he lay on his deathbed, he handed the legendary sword to his son, ensuring it would pass through generations.

Thus ended the reign of Meriden, the mighty warrior king of Champa, but his legacy lived on through his descendants and the blade that bore the will of Purushottam.

XII

The end

One day, Natasha called Dravin and said, "It's been three months of C-C-C. I think we should do it today."

Dravin replied, "Surveillance checking, right? Let's do it. You have to come today."

Everyone was assembled, and Dravin stood up to address them. "Hello, everyone. Today, we conduct C-C-C—our surveillance check. If anything unnoticed remains, we will catch it. The wrongdoer may be among us, or it may be one of your friends. I won't point fingers yet, but I ask everyone to follow instructions. Before you leave, all electronic access will be revoked. Gather your belongings and head straight home. The military is already here, guarding the building. If anyone tries anything, I will be notified immediately. So, I request everyone to leave respectfully, including department heads—except for myself, the VAI officials like Natasha, and Ame Govert officials. Now, please exit peacefully. Thank you."

Nihal and Mahi grew tense. A mail had been sent to everyone stating that the VAI function would be suspended for three days due to C-C-C. This made them even more anxious. As all cameras were checked—except for Dravin's and Natasha's—Dravin was about to leave without checking, but Natasha insisted. To their shock, they found Nihal and Mahi inside Dravin's cabin. Their homes were immediately raided, and they were taken to VAI headquarters.

There, they were interrogated brutally. After a long ordeal, they were finally seated, and Dravin asked the first question, "How are you guys?"

Nihal smirked and replied, "It's Nihal, your loved one," blowing a flying kiss to Dravin and everyone present.

Laughing, Nihal grabbed Mahi's hand, suddenly channeling a mysterious energy. He shouted, and a surge of power coursed through his hands. In an instant, he shattered the roof and escaped with Mahi.

Dravin explained the incident to the team. One member spoke up, "I know how he escaped. There was a man named Meriden, whose sword had immense power, including teleportation. That sword was linked to VA because Justin's forefathers ruled beside the Kingdom of Champa. This is all connected. Meriden was the King of Champa, and he received the sword as a blessing from his father, uncle, and guru. Only he could change its rules. Since his death, the rules have remained unchanged. I suspect Nihal has gained powers from Meriden's sword. We need to investigate this. What is Justin's surname?"

Dravin replied, "Radin."

The member gasped. "We've been so blind. He's literally of royal blood. Radin was the name of Meriden's father! My mother used to tell me these stories—her ancestors lived in the Kingdom of Champa. First, we must study the history. Then, using our VA knowledge, we'll analyze Nihal's strengths, weaknesses, and abilities."

Dravin instructed the team to compile a report with their findings. After meticulous research, they tracked Nihal's every move and formulated a strategy.

Dravin then used his powers to send a message to Nihal:

DEATH BATTLE. I CHALLENGE YOU. NO RULES, NO CHEATING, NO THIRD-PARTY INVOLVEMENT. WHOEVER DIES, DIES. LET'S FIGHT. EXPECTING YOU TO BE FAST.

Nihal responded immediately, summoning himself to the borders of Kansas. Both warriors harnessed their powers and began levitating in the sky. The battle commenced. Dravin struck first, hitting Nihal in the face. Nihal retaliated with the same force. They exchanged punches, kicks, and slaps before each grabbed a 90mm iron rod and started beating each other mercilessly. After two hours of relentless fighting, they finally drew their ultimate weapons—Meriden's Sword and the Vector Axe.

They stabbed each other repeatedly, blood spilling as they fought to the death. Then, their weapons clashed, triggering a massive explosion that obliterated both weapons—and themselves. Dravin and Nihal were reduced to ashes.

Far away, in a celestial realm, a divine figure observed the battle. The God turned to his son and said,

"मम पुत्रः, पश्यतु अत्र शस्त्राणां युद्धम् अभवत्, तत् प्रत्येकस्य समस्यायाः समाप्तिः आसीत्, इदानीं सर्वे शान्तिपूर्वकं निर्गन्तव्यं, अहं एतत् युद्धं कृतवान् यतः; अहं शस्त्राणां प्रयोगं समाप्तुम् इच्छामि स्म, वयं जानीमः यत् ये जनाः वेक्टर-अक्षं प्रयुक्तवन्तः ते मृताः इति, परन्तु मेरिडेन् इत्यस्य खड्गः कः इति भवान् स्मर्यते वा, यः सर्वैः न प्रयुक्तः आसीत्, सः केवलं रेडिन्/मेरिडेन् इत्यस्य पीढ्याभिः एव प्रयुक्तः आसीत्, एकदिवसे अहं कथाम् अपि वर्णितवान्, मया स्मर्यते, इदानीं वयं शान्तिपूर्वकं जीवामः, जनाः च शान्तिपूर्वकं जीवन्ति।"

(Translation: "Oh, my son, behold this battle of weapons. It has ended every problem. Now, all should depart peacefully. I allowed this battle because I wished to end the use of weapons. We know that those who wielded the Vector Axe perished, but do you remember Meriden's Sword? It was not meant for all—it was wielded only by the lineage of Radin/Meriden. One day, I even narrated this story. Now, we shall live in peace, and so shall the people.")

The God's son replied, "सः पिता इव अस्ति वा, या; मया स्मर्यते यदा त्वं कथां कथयसि।"

(Translation: "Oh! Is it like that, Father? Yes, I remember when you told the story.")

Thus, the legend of the Vector Axe and Meriden's Sword came to an end. According to divine wisdom,

"यदि जनानां कृते शस्त्राणि निर्मीयन्ते, अन्यम् अपि निर्मीयन्ते, यदि जनाः उभयोः शस्त्राणां उपयोगं कुर्वन्ति; शस्त्राणां समाप्तिः भविष्यति, अयं नियमः सर्वैः न ज्ञातः स्यात्, परन्तु अस्माकं ग्रन्थेषु अस्य उल्लेखः अस्ति।"

(Translation: "If one weapon is forged, another will follow. If both are used, they will lead to the end of all weapons. This rule may not be known to all, but it is recorded in our ancient texts.")

And so, the cycle of destruction was broken, and peace was restored.

Conclusion

The battle between Dravin and Nihal was the last of its kind. Their fight, fueled by history, power, and personal grudges, ended with both of them reduced to ashes. The great weapons—Meriden's Sword and the Vector Axe—were destroyed forever, ensuring that no one else could wield their deadly power.

As the gods watched, they decided that this was the final war of weapons. No more swords, no more axes—only peace. The people who once lived in fear of these powers were now free. No longer would battles shape their lives, and no longer would ancient legacies control their future.

Justin Radin, who unknowingly carried the bloodline of Meriden, realized the importance of these events. He decided to record everything, making sure future generations knew the story. This was not just a tale of war, but a lesson—that power without control leads to destruction, and that some fights should never happen.

And so, the world moved forward. The battle became a legend, a warning to all: true strength is not in weapons, but in wisdom.

Postscript

As the final pages of this story turn, the echoes of battle, destiny, and sacrifice remain. The tale of power, legacy, and fate intertwined through generations serves as a reminder that history is never truly forgotten. The clash of the Meriden Sword and the Vector Axe was not just a battle between warriors but a testament to the consequences of wielding power.

In the end, the world moves forward, carrying the lessons of the past. The legends of Dravin, Nihal, and the Radin lineage will remain in the hearts of those who seek the truth. Was this truly the end of their story, or is it just another chapter in a never-ending cycle of history? The answer lies in the hands of those who choose to remember.

Afterword

The journey of this story has been one of mystery, power, and fate. From the shadows of forgotten history to the clash of legendary warriors, every event led to an inevitable conclusion. The conflict between Dravin and Nihal was not just about power but about legacy—about the burden of carrying a history that shapes the future.

In the end, as the Meriden Sword and Vector Axe met their destruction, it was a reminder that all power comes at a cost. But beyond battles and destinies, the true message lies in understanding one's place in the grand scheme of things. Are we bound by the past, or do we have the power to change the course of the future?

As readers, you have walked this journey alongside the characters, feeling their struggles, witnessing their choices, and seeing the consequences unfold. But every ending is also a beginning. Perhaps one day, new stories will emerge from the ashes of this tale—stories yet to be written, yet to be lived.

Until then, let this story remain in memory, a tale of fate, courage, and the power that lies within us all.

Epilogue

The battlefield lay silent, a stark contrast to the chaos it had witnessed. The once-mighty clash of warriors had long since faded, leaving only the wind to stir the remnants of a war that had shaped the fate of many. The ground, scorched and cracked, bore the weight of history—where blood had once soaked the earth, only dust remained.

The Vector Axe, the very weapon that had been at the heart of this long struggle, now rested undisturbed in the depths of its final resting place. No hands would wield it again, no wars would be fought over its power. It remained a relic of an era that had come to an end, a silent testament to those who had sacrificed everything in its name.

The Kingdom of Champa, though battered, stood resilient. Its golden temples, once darkened by war, slowly reclaimed their former glory under the watchful hands of its people. Walls were rebuilt, roads repaired, and life, after so much turmoil, began to bloom again. The voices that once cried out in anguish were now filled with laughter, the shadows of war retreating as light returned to the land.

For those who had survived, the memories of battle would never fully fade. The weight of their losses, the faces of those who had fallen, remained etched in their hearts. Yet, as time moved forward, so did they. Some found solace in rebuilding what had been lost, others in sharing the stories of what had been endured. The war had taken much, but it had not stolen everything.

Legends, once spoken with urgency and fear, became mere stories whispered under the glow of lanterns. The names of warriors, once known across lands, began to fade into history. And perhaps that was how it should be—war was never meant to be eternal. The victors did not celebrate, nor did the defeated seek revenge. There was no lingering prophecy, no hidden force waiting in the shadows. Only peace.

The winds carried away the last echoes of war, sweeping across the quiet ruins, the rebuilt homes, and the untouched Vector Axe. No longer a weapon of destruction, no longer a symbol of power. Just a reminder of what had been.

The battle was over. The story had ended. And for the first time in a long time, the world could finally rest.

Glossary

1. Vector Axe – A legendary weapon of immense power, known to shift the balance of fate with its wielder.

2. Meriden Sword – A mystical blade said to possess divine energy, used to counteract the Vector Axe's destructive force.

3. Kingdom of Champa – An ancient and prosperous land filled with golden temples, powerful rulers, and secrets buried in time.

4. The Awakening – A pivotal moment when a warrior or entity discovers their hidden strength, altering the course of destiny.

5. The Final Duel – The ultimate battle that determines the fate of kingdoms and warriors alike.

6. The Ruins of the Past – The remnants of great civilizations lost to war, holding untold secrets and forgotten powers.

7. The Shadow Figure – A mysterious entity lurking in the darkness, watching and waiting for the right moment to strike.

8. Tornadoes of Kansas – Natural forces of destruction symbolizing chaos, fate, and the unpredictable nature of battle.

9. The Lost Warriors – Legends of fighters who disappeared in battle, their spirits rumored to roam the earth.

10. Supernatural Runes – Ancient inscriptions found on sacred weapons and ruins, believed to unlock hidden abilities.

11. The Scorched Earth – A battlefield burned and ruined by war, where life struggles to return.

12. The Golden Temples – Sacred places within the Kingdom of Champa, known for their spiritual significance and historical importance.

13. The Cave of Fate – A hidden sanctuary where the most powerful weapons and artifacts of history remain untouched.

14. The Ancient Prophecy – A long-lost prediction that foretells the rise and fall of great warriors and kingdoms.

15. The Silent Battlefield – The eerie stillness after a war, where only memories and echoes remain.

16. The Guardian of the Axe – A being tasked with protecting the Vector Axe from falling into the wrong hands.

17. The River of Destiny – A mystical river said to flow through time, showing glimpses of the past, present, and future.

18. The Unseen War – Battles fought in the shadows, where political intrigue and hidden agendas shape history.

19. The Cursed Blade – A weapon forged in darkness, bringing ruin to those who wield it.

20. The Eternal Watcher – A figure or force that observes history unfold, guiding or manipulating events in secrecy.

www.ingramcontent.com/pod-product-compliance
Lightning Source LLC
Chambersburg PA
CBHW020453160726
47991CB00007B/2634